Virtue

The Gamer's Girlfriend

Ida Brady

Proofreading by Norma Gambini
Cover design by DAZED Designs
Formatting by Ebony McKenna

www.idabrady.com

To Team Brida,
For all the love, group hugs and chocolate.

To all my Regency romancers out there,
I simply couldn't resist.

Chapter One

S avannah stroked the spine of the book, a smile playing at her lips.

It was her umpteenth time reading *Love and Honor*, a classic nineteenth-century romance and all she could think about was why the Duke of Maddern didn't bend Miss Collins over his desk and show her just how proud he could be.

She could picture him in the library now, stalking towards Emmaline, demanding she lift her skirts.

Her imagination beckoned along with her desire.

The Duke followed Miss Collins into the library, his cock straining against his breeches. He shut the door behind him firmly, the sharp click reverberating through the empty room. Time was limited. Flustered and uncertain, Emmaline's chaperone, an older, unmarried relative, had accepted the Earl's offer to dance.

He owed Lord Stanton a great sum for the diversion.

The moon was particularly bright this evening, piercing through the windows, illuminating the beauty of the woman before him. All softness had faded, though the years had not been unkind. There was a haunting beauty to her visage, a sadness that shadowed her graceful movements. For as long as he could remember, she had conducted herself as a lady. Indeed, she was, if not for the inconvenience of her father's station, a lady in every respect.

She would always be so in his mind.

Was he in his cups, or were her lips an even darker shade of peony than he remembered? Even with her brow pinched and her mouth downturned, she stirred a long-forgotten feeling inside.

He knew it was not right to be alone with her in this fashion. Even still, he would chase this woman to the most exotic, far-off continents.

"I've been thinking about you since Mrs. Perryweather's play."

He watched as one round shoulder lifted in nonchalance. Despite the casual gesture, her eyes shimmered with unspoken thoughts.

Once he had been privy to such musings, but no longer.

"Is that so, Your Grace? I thought you were rather occupied."

Maddern had been overrun by young ladies eager to make his acquaintance. He was quite a catch according to the meddling mammas. Yet not one of the simpering ingénues had stirred his appetite.

He knew what they said. After all, he was a duke with a considerable fortune. A duty, he found, that was akin to a hangman's noose. Maddern was weary of doing what was expected. None of it mattered if he didn't get what he truly desired.

The woman standing before him.

Miss Emmaline Collins.

She was stubborn and impertinent. Bold in her manner. And she harbored a hatred for him that had not dissipated over time. He intended to bring her to heel, perhaps over his bended knee. The image was too illicit to fathom, but once it had taken up residence in his head, he was determined to make it a reality.

"Don't play coy with me. I am not a fool," Maddern rumbled.

"One must not laugh at the noble Duke. He is, after all, such a jovial, candid man."

"Lift those skirts, wench, and I will show you the real meaning of candid."

If this were R-rated, the Duke would have most certainly done just that. He would have stuck his tongue down Emmaline's throat and given her the banging of her virgin life. Which would then lead to a lot of sexy, horny frolics in closets and dark rooms.

But if *Love and Honor* were R-rated, then not only would Emmaline Collins and William Barnet, the Duke of Maddern, have had sex already, she would, after the fact, naturally hate him even more for licking her *button*. Especially as he rejected her all those years ago.

Emmaline could not help that her mother was born a lady but that her father was—gasp—a barrister. She was in every respect a gentleman's daughter, but simply a poor one. It was a grand offence by the *ton*'s standards. If it were not for her aunt's, the Duchess of Carrington's, generosity to her nieces, she would not have met him. Or fallen in love. Or had her heart broken when Maddern chose to obey his parents instead of pursuing her.

Savannah had it all written out in her head. Hell, she couldn't help but fantasize about it whenever she read her all-time favorite classic. And since this was her hundredth read of *Love and Honor*, she'd had plenty of time to come up with her scandalous side-plot.

She didn't need much incentive in that department.

The reason she was drawn to the classics was because there was so much *restraint*. It was almost maddening to read about characters falling in love but still bound by societal rules. She knew all about living a restricted life. Every morning she was thankful she was now free.

Savannah stretched out on the bed, her mind wired even though her body was fatigued. She liked having bits and pieces of work, but bartending on top of her shifts at the library was starting to take its toll.

Despite her boyfriend's income, she was adamant that she pay her own bills. She was all too aware of what happened when people you loved turned on you. But she couldn't think about her parents now. At twenty-four, Savannah had a solid amount of savings, and she was adamant to never rely on anyone ever again.

"Fuck, no!" Arcas suddenly cried from the other room. "Stun him, you moron!"

Her boyfriend was gaming—had been ever since she'd arrived home. She figured he was in the midst of a raid. Arcas was not only a hardcore gamer, but he actually made money from the thousands of people who paid to watch him. It was no wonder; he was fucking good at it. Those hands were a hot commodity—in and out of the bedroom.

Talk about hero material.

While she enjoyed getting lost in *The Realm* every now and then, she wasn't in the mood to try and hunt for the dragon who had claimed one of the maidens. Yeah, she could join him. But tonight, she wanted something else.

Tonight, her illicit fantasies beckoned.

She wouldn't say she was addicted to sex, but she had a higher libido than most, one which she couldn't ignore . . . or wouldn't. It had made growing up in a super strict, conservative household very confusing. Savannah had tried for years as a teenager to just pretend it wasn't there, but the desire didn't go away. Instead, it built up, burning through her body, consuming her every action until she relented.

Why should she ignore something that gave her so much pleasure? Not just sex, but the pre-sex: the wonderful daydreaming, the tension in her body that kept her company when she was busy stacking shelves or waiting tables.

On the nights when Arcas was raiding, she had her assortment of devices to give her the release she craved. He called it her toy box, and the description was pretty apt. It was a gorgeous nineteenth-century-style chest made of dark mahogany and lined with velvet.

It was the only semi-precious thing she owned, her books coming a close second.

Lube, vibrators, whips, the occasional dirty magazine, it was all there in her sex box. She would delve into it before the night was through.

Savannah lifted the book off her chest and flipped to the confrontation scene where Emmaline rebuked the Duke for the hurt he had caused. The spine yielded with ease; it was one of her favorite chapters.

Maddern was a tight-lipped bastard. She could picture him, tall and dark, his arrogantly straight nose and even straighter posture looking down on Emmaline. Lusting after her, even when he was aware of the restrictions of a gentleman.

"I apologize. I was but a boy then." The Duke's aloof manner belied his tone, now steeped in regret. Or so it would seem. She had been wronged by His Grace once before.

"Yet man enough to know how to break a woman's heart," she replied.

Emmaline was blind to all else but the bitter ache in her chest. He had chosen duty, the dictates of his family and title over her. He had not the courage to love her enough. Or had not enough love to find the courage. Neither offered comfort.

"My family's fortune has not changed, Your Grace. Nor has my situation."

"Time has afforded me some wisdom."

"Is that so? It is of no consequence to me."

"That is obvious."

"I remain a spinster. Any connection to me only prolongs my pain further. If you are the gentleman society claims you to be, then pray, leave me alone, Your Grace."

. . .

If Savannah were writing the novel, Maddern would be doing everything he could to impress Emmaline. He wouldn't allow another man to touch her.

In her version, Maddern would be inviting Emmaline to a social gathering at his estate. He would be sociable and kind—all to please her. In doing so, he would find her a willing and eager partner for a romp in the library. One in which Emmaline would feel . . .

Savannah closed the book. Unbuttoning her pink pajama top, she ran her hand along her stomach, the skin soft and yielding. She pinched her sides, raking her nails down her hips before slipping her hands inside her shorts.

But she was getting ahead of herself. There needed to be an incident before the library that would spark their dalliance.

How would the seduction begin?

Chapter Two

I t was sinful. Scandalous. But by far, it was the most thrilling experience of her sheltered life.

For Emmaline Collins, one of four daughters of a middle-class barrister, pleasure was not a luxury she could afford. Never mind that her mother, Lady Elizabeth, was the daughter of an earl. In the eyes of the ton, her father's profession was not worth a groat.

With the exception of one man. The Duke of Maddern.

Just the thought of his name sent a burning heat through her body.

She had woken aroused. The throbbing ache between her thighs persisted despite her walk to the greenhouse.

The heady, heavy scent of the earth, the rich aroma of the flowers, only increased her desire. She was very much alone, surrounded by exotic plants and in need of . . . release.

Having informed her maid of her intended direction, she had donned her shawl and ventured off to the gardens on the estate, very much alone. No servants. No staff. No family.

But she had accepted the invitation to stay with her aunt, drawn by a secret, foolish desire to meet the Duke once again. Yes, seeing His Grace after all these years had been shocking. It had stirred a long-forgotten need inside her and with it, a wave of memories.

Here, at her aunt and uncle's estate, was where they once played as children. Innocent of the harsh dictates of society.

This was where she had given him her heart, only to have it ripped apart.

Emmaline found a garden seat tucked away in the greenhouse and settled into it. A steady ache had accompanied her since she crossed paths with him again, not that they had spoken. But a look, a glance across the crowded room of Lady Huntington's ball was all it took. She was ablaze with need and unable to embroider the feeling away. Painting, singing, conversations with her sister, none of them diverted her in the manner she craved.

The stirring began. There. Just there.

A heavy, pulsing ache. One she had not experienced before. At least, not at this scale.

Emmaline bit her lip, casting her eyes around the flowers just coming into bloom.

There was something blossoming inside her. It

had been there since she had met the haughty Duke of Maddern, her long-ago love.

Certain she was alone, hidden by the lush, verdant foliage, Emmaline lifted her skirts and pressed down on the spot between her legs.

"Oh!" A jolt passed through her. She retracted her hand as if she had touched a burning flame.

Her heart thrummed in her chest, and after a few breathless moments, she replaced her fingers, this time increasing the pressure. The new and wicked sensation raced through her, but she continued boldly. She did not know what was happening, but in truth, it was exhilarating.

She moved her hips, searching. She could not be sure what was missing, but a different feeling flooded her now. A distinct emptiness a little lower than her hand.

Her womb was barren. Her virginity intact. And when an arrogant face in her mind stared back at her, she quivered.

Emmaline's fingers flew now, racing towards the clawing, greedy ache driving her to distraction. Perspiration gathered beneath her stays. Her cheeks felt flushed. A musky, heavy scent punctuated the air.

Then his face returned. Emmaline closed her eyes, but still he persisted.

Broad, strong shoulders. A disdainful expression. Eyes as green and glittering as the finest jewels of all the land.

The need inside her grew. A heavy, strange wet-ness pooled between her thighs.

Emmaline dipped her finger lower, gathering the slick moisture, rubbing it against the spot that left her breathless.

She was wanton for such an act. Even more so for desiring a man beyond her reach.

She pictured his dark head lowering, his mouth fixed on hers . . .

Emmaline gasped, fingers flying, trembling, straining for what, she did not understand. And when his mouth explored her neck, then lower, she cried out, breaking and tumbling. Shaking, Emma-line sunk into the latticework at her back, fascinated by what had just occurred. There was a wetness be-neath her and a thrumming inside.

She drifted, the pounding blood in her ears sub-siding, her body relaxed and loose. Her hand rested on her mound as she contemplated trying it again.

A low creaking noise punctuated the silence.

Her eyes flew open as footsteps approached.

Emmaline started. Dazed, she could not lower her skirts; she was shocked and rendered mute by the tall, imposing figure before her.

The Duke stopped short, his green eyes, usually distant, heated.

"You best rearrange your skirts. Your maid will be upon us shortly."

Emmaline followed his command, mortified at

the intrusion. How much had he seen? A furious stain marked her cheeks. Everything.

Of all times to be inconvenienced. Of all people to happen upon her.

Her heart pounded like a wild rabbit, and Emmaline debated the best way to proceed.

"I wished to call on your aunt and uncle."

"They are out."

"That is clear enough."

Her thoughts raced. Still, she kept her eyes averted.

"Do you make it a habit to lift your skirts in such a fashion?" His deep voice was strained.

Emmaline's eyes flew to his face. Shock at his bold response made her stand.

"That is an entirely inappropriate thing to ask."

"It is an entirely appropriate question given the state I found you."

"Indeed, I am uncertain as to why you are even here . . . Your Grace."

The Duke frowned and memories of a young boy hovered before her. A boy who had broken her heart. Her dreams.

He stepped forward. "I wished to see you, but I found you . . . occupied."

Emmaline's color deepened. The wicked smile that danced in his eyes was wholly inappropriate.

As was this private conversation.

. . .

Savannah was greedy for her own release. The wicked fantasy that played in her mind catapulted her desire to a new level. She crawled over to her sex box, taking out her Rabbit. She applied lube on the shaft, eager to have her Greedy Girl thrusting into her.

She could picture the Duke dismissing the lady's maid, kneeling in front of Emmaline even as he lifted her skirts, feasting on her wet juices. Pleasuring her all over again.

Who cared if he hadn't thought she was fit to marry all those years ago? He wanted her now, desperate for a taste of her sweet wares.

Savannah moaned, sliding the vibrator inside, feeling the delicious moment of resistance before her body yielded. The sensations on her clit were enough to get her off, but she wanted to feel like she was being fucked, and the thrusting shaft hit the spot, over and over, heightened by the fantasies inside her mind.

Oh yes, the Duke would undress her completely, toying with Emmaline's breasts, fusing his mouth to hers in a kiss that would compel him to deflower her. To be the only man to taste her.

She panted, knowing she was close. Her Rabbit pumped inside her, a steady rhythmic pressure, while her clit throbbed from the stimulation. She arched back on the bed, straining, writhing, waiting with bated breath for the small swirling jolts of pleasure to engulf her whole.

The Duke would then free himself of his breeches and sink his cock inside her, pummeling into Emmaline like a stallion rutting a mare. And she would love it, clawing his back, begging for more.

Harder. Faster. Deeper.

Savannah cried out, hips jerking as she lost control. The luxurious sensations flooded her clit, radiating through her pussy, racing over her body until she was spent.

Oh yes. This was *her* pleasure.

Chapter Three

"I've figured it out."

"What?"

"The restless feeling of late."

"Ah. That." Arcas took a sip of whiskey, rolling the balls of ice around in his glass. "Shoot."

"I keep thinking about how I grew up. All those restrictions and rules made for a sheltered adolescence. But I feel like college didn't give me as many experiences as I'd hoped and I'm wanting to explore."

"And now that you're no longer in contact with your parents—thank fuck—you have the freedom to do it."

"I do . . ." She didn't want to focus on the conversation that had essentially severed any ties she had to her family. It had been painful yet necessary.

It had happened not long after she met Arcas, who, in his easy, worldly way, had offered her comfort and advice. Not to mention amazing sex.

"Hey, don't go back there." Arcas' knuckles softly brushed her cheek.

"I finally got rid of the box."

"Ahh."

Savannah gripped the cold glass. "I know it was the right thing to do, the right time, but I didn't expect it to make me feel so . . ."

"Lost?"

"Free. And maybe guilty."

"You're getting rid of those fucked-up reminders. It's bound to leave you a little guilty at first, not that any of their shit is your fault. Van, this was the right thing to do. Letting go, throwing out those reminders will help."

"I know it's going to take some time to feel totally okay, but today was liberating. It's unlocked this invisible barrier I've been keeping in my mind. And I'm sick of the restrictions, of not living up to their expectations."

Savannah drank the last of her cocktail, contemplating another round. She had tried so hard to be the good girl they had wanted, the good *Christian* girl who would do as she was told.

Emotions were frowned upon.

Sexual liberty was forbidden.

Obedience was key.

By the time she had left for college, practically every book, film, and pastime was a sin of the flesh. Corruptible. Condemnable. Punished.

Throwing out the remaining flotsam and jetsam

from her past should have left her feeling bereft, but what she had experienced was a surge of relief.

She hadn't thought how stifling those objects had been. Even though they were tucked away in the small shoebox at the back of her closet, it had been a presence in her life for too long.

Today she had the courage to throw it out.

No more bible. No more coercive letters. None of the Evangelical paraphernalia that she had been forced to believe for most of her life.

But there was one thing she wouldn't throw out, one thing she couldn't: an image of her and her older brother. They were young, only just in school, cuddling their mother and father and smiling with such joy it made her heart ache. It was the only photo she kept of her parents—before they had subscribed to the Evangelical way of life. Before her whole world had come crashing down.

Savannah shivered.

She wasn't a child anymore. Or hell, even a confused teenager. She'd finally broken free of the church and her parents' abuse. She refused to go through life stifling her feelings or desires.

No more.

This need inside her had been building for years now. Being with Arcas, living with him, had given her the confidence, the reassurance that she wouldn't be burning in hellfire if she succumbed to temptation. And Lord help her, that need for more had only increased of late.

What had started off as a casual thing a year ago turned into a proper relationship. She had noticed Arcas' wheelchair that night while she was waiting tables at the restaurant, and the fact that he was giving her all the interested signals. She hadn't questioned the technicalities of sex with a paraplegic when he had invited her back to his place. She hadn't had room in her overheated brain to think at all once he stripped off her clothes.

And while there was a decade between them, it wasn't ever an issue. A year into their relationship and the only major change had been Savannah's decision to agree to move into his inner-city apartment. It was close to work and meant that she wasn't travelling across town at odd hours of the night.

Arcas wheeled closer. "So you want a bit of a thrill?"

Savannah smiled, aware of what he was doing, and thankful of it. "Yes. I'm sick of living my life according to a set of invisible rules or rebelling just for the sake of it. I want to experience as many endorphins as I can. It isn't the vodka talking either, though hell knows I've had more than my share of martinis."

"Talk it out." Arcas stroked her neck; grasping the back of it, he kneaded out the kinks and aches.

"Hmmm." She loved his hands. They never failed to hit the right spot. "What was I saying?" She opened her eyes, now a little heavier.

"Endorphins," he prompted, lips curving.

"Yep . . . I want them."

They were sitting in a bar a few blocks from their apartment, their regular late-night haunt in the heart of Melbourne's CBD. It was the perfect post-work venue. It wasn't too loud, or at this time of night, too crowded either.

"So, endorphins. Like the ones coursing through your body right now?" He increased the pressure on her neck. He was a sexy fucker, especially when he teased her, his eyes suggesting more than he ever said. All that messy dark hair, his angular jaw . . . No wonder she was distracted.

"Mmm."

His intensity was a perfect contrast to her playful, carefree personality. So when he toyed with her as he did now, her heart did a little fluttery dance.

Arcas withdrew his hand, bringing her back to the conversation.

"I can't be massaged all day, every day, can I?"

"Well . . ." He grinned. "Are you looking for mad endorphins from jumping out of a plane, or more along the lines of 'I just bit into a delicious slice of mud cake?'"

Savannah drummed her fingers on the table. "Cake is good. Planes bad. I want the thrill to be sexual. I want to have as many different orgasms as I can in as many different ways."

"Now you're talking."

She pressed her lips together, suffocating the smile. She was trying to be serious. Maybe.

"I mean it. I want to really explore my sexuality."

"You know I'm open to anything and everything. That includes adding a few more people to our little love club. Bec asked me if you're interested."

"Did she? I haven't been with a woman since college."

"She's been asking since last year's Christmas party."

"I'm up for it. Now I'm getting distracted."

"And aroused?"

"Always . . . I want to broaden my horizons, have nothing off limits."

"Like a sex challenge?"

"Ooh. I like that. A sex challenge. Fuck, yeah."

Arcas stroked the back of her hand. "You could even journal about it online, really kick up the accountability."

"Ugh, you promised you wouldn't bring up the 'B' word."

"There's nothing wrong with blogging."

Savannah wrinkled her nose. "It's so ten years ago."

"And yet, the world still turns."

Savannah huffed, downing the last of her pornstar martini. "So where do I start?"

"Trawl the internet, see what tickles your fancy

or what doesn't, then experiment. And write about it. You do words good," he imitated in his best cave man voice. "Try it out, see what works. I'm man enough to be okay with you wanting a functioning cock in your sex life, Van."

"You've said that many times."

"Just reminding you, there's nothing off limits."

She placed a hand on his. "Do you miss it?"

Arcas dipped his finger in his whiskey glass, toying with the amber liquid. "At times. The same with my legs. But if I still had use of them, I wouldn't be here, with you. I've built a life that I love. It isn't where I thought I'd end up when I was twenty-five, but earning big money and having a hot girlfriend has somewhat assuaged the melancholy."

"You know I think you're pretty amazing, right?"

"No pity. That was the number one rule."

"I'm not. I never have. But I do think I'm one lucky 'hot girlfriend' to have you."

"Like my ego needs stroking. But honestly, Van, I've been living this way for ten years. Sure, I'll never go skiing the same way or mountain hiking or any of that shit, but I've made peace with that."

"I've only ever known you as you are."

"A handsome fucker wanting to take his girl-friend home?"

Savannah loved his honesty. His liberal views about sex and relationships were unlike a lot of men she had previously dated, who only wanted to possess her, to hold on tighter. It was probably why their casual fling had progressed into a steady, committed relationship.

"You *are* pretty to look at."

"Damned with faint praise. Look, I'm comfortable enough with my sexuality to try new things." He tugged at a strand of her dark brown hair, unbound and flowing down her back. "So as a sacrifice, I'll offer to be a willing participant in your sex challenge."

"How magnanimous of you."

"Then you can set up a Patreon for people to pay you for your sexual insights."

Savannah shook her head. "Not sure that's what it's meant for. Plus, nobody's going to pay me to write about a year's worth of orgasms."

Arcas took her chin in his hand, leaning forward. "You're wrong, Van. A lot of people would pay to share in your pleasure. In case I haven't told you, you're a fucking goddess, so don't forget it."

Savannah licked her lips, desire shooting straight to her nether regions. She kissed him, floating on a cloud of need. They were both a little breathless by the time she pulled back.

Arcas' green eyes glittered wickedly. His hand brushed the side of her torso, stoking her body, igniting her fantasies.

"The goddess wants to go home now."

She had research to do.

Chapter Four

Savannah panted, body slick with sweat, arms trembling, a butt plug rammed in her hole. Arcas lay beneath her, gripping her ass. His silver tongue hit the spot that always sent her body into overdrive.

She had been eager for this threesome ever since he had mentioned it. But having Bec here, with her back against the wall, legs splayed as she toyed with her pussy was better than any daydream. The long, thick dildo disappeared as she pleasured herself, hips rolling, mouth parted.

She toyed with Bec's nipples then flicked her tongue over the dark tips, grinning as her moans deepened. Savannah feasted on her breasts, grazing her teeth along the soft sides, sliding her tongue around the darkened flesh.

She ground her pussy on Arcas' face, rubbing her clit back and forth, desperate for the release he was holding back. The release she kept at bay. She cried out when his open palm slapped her ass and goosebumps travelled down her thighs. She was beginning to crave the pleasure-pain, to hold her breath in anticipation of the next strike.

A flash of silver distracted her. Bec reached for something that looked like two small pliers, holding them out in her hand. "Care to try?"

"Are they clamps?"

"They are. We can take them off any time if it's not your thing."

"I'm game." Savannah licked her lips, watching as Bec tweaked her own nipple, pinching the areola between the cold metal clamps. She gasped when Bec reached out and did the same to hers. The silver chain dangled heavily between them, tethering their desire.

"Oh." Savannah felt the jolt through her breasts, shooting down to her clit.

The pinching pressure, the delightful squeezing of her nipple left her flushed and shaking. She had suppressed this need within her for so long, but now that she was succumbing to it, now that she was submitting to the wonderous exploration of her body, she was consumed by the glorious rush of her own arousal. The heady thrill of something new. She felt bold and daring and fuck it, sexy as hell.

Savannah tugged Bec closer, kissing her with a desperation that would not subside. Her soft and supple body glistened with sweat. Her scent, floral and creamy and so utterly womanly beckoned.

"Fuck, that's hot," Savannah muttered, feeling the weight of the chain that linked them. "I'm close," she whispered.

"You want to try the second clamp?"

She nodded in assent, bucking when Bec secured it. The pressure, the shock of it, radiated through her body. A wild desperation to come seized her now. Savannah kissed her, tongues gliding, dancing, thrusting, until the pulsing in her clit was almost painful. She chased that feeling, straining until she reached the point of surrender.

Rocking over Arcas, she gripped Bec's hips and cried out, clenching her thighs together, body suspended in need. Arcas' tongue thrust inside her pussy, his thumb working over her clit, driving her hard to orgasm.

She chased the high, racing headlong into the pleasure that pummeled through her. She could barely breathe, lost, and consumed by its force. Breaking, she sobbed in victory, shuddering in release.

Savannah drifted, enjoying the after-shocks, the piecing together of her mind and body that only moments prior had been rendered in two. Taking her time, she unclipped the clamps then rolled on her back.

Being with a woman in college had been an act of rebellion, a way to distance herself as much as possible from her parents' rules. Being with a woman as a grown adult wanting to explore her sexual interests was even more satisfying.

Through heavy-lidded eyes, she watched as Bec straddled Arcas, toying with him until he groaned. She had a long tongue and used it well, trailing patterns along his mouth then around his nipples, licking and sucking, exploring every inch of his body.

Savannah sat up, shifting closer to her boyfriend. Arcas palmed her breasts, tweaking her still-engorged nipples, grinning when she shuddered. She captured his hand then slowly inserted his index finger into her mouth.

He cursed silently, mouth parting, eyes greedy.

She continued biting and sucking his fingers, massaging each digit, taking her sweet time.

"I want to watch you getting fucked," Arcas demanded.

"Always delaying gratification."

His grin was relaxed. "Tastes better that way."

"Uh huh."

"I brought my strap-on." Bec shifted off the bed, grinning. "I always come prepared."

Savannah smiled, leaning over Arcas, kissing him in slow, languid strokes. She loved that they could indulge in this together, that their relationship was secure and yet flexible.

He reached around, pinching her ass, then removed the butt plug. "I want to see your ass getting a pounding."

"Ask and you shall receive." She smirked.

Savannah lay back on the bed as Bec applied lube to the double-ended device, inserting the longer end inside her own pussy.

"This shorter end is for you, Van. I figured we can start slow. Once you're comfortable I can use the vibrator function to really hit the spot." She wiggled the black remote beside her before placing a pillow underneath Savannah's ass.

Bec positioned her hips, fingering Savannah's hole, applying more lube until she moaned for more. She lifted her legs up, resting them on Bec's shoulders, heart thrumming as the tip of the dildo nudged her ass. She slowed down her breathing, relaxing her body as Bec entered her.

Savannah played with her clit, slow, easy strokes, building her need. Inch by inch, she was impaled. The pressure was immense, a thick, heavy intrusion that only increased with every thrust. She was being wonderfully filled, but it wasn't enough.

Bec whimpered, fucking her ass in slow, drawn-out moves. When she turned on the vibrator, at the lowest setting, Savannah gasped.

With each stroke, she wanted more, aching for her pussy to be fucked, too. She reached for her dildo then groaned when Arcas' hand gripped hers.

"Allow me."

He bit her nipples, still sensitive from the clamps, before taking her dildo and trailing it along her curves, stopping at the sensitive area on her hip before roaming down to her shaved pussy. Savannah brought her knees back to her chest, then with bated breath, she waited.

Arcas hovered, torturing her.

"Don't play games."

His grin was filled with smug satisfaction. "Or what?" he teased, thrusting into her in one smooth motion.

Savannah jerked at the force. "Fuck!"

Slowly he withdrew, in and out, over and over, building her need, teasing her until she was hot and slick with sweat. Bec and Arcas rhythmically plundered, and the vibrating dildo in her ass only magnified her pleasure; the sensation was unlike anything she had experienced before. Savannah was stretched and filled and wonderfully consumed. She was a quivering mess, greedily lusting for more with every stroke.

When Arcas bit down on her neck, she sobbed, half-crazed with desire.

"I'm gonna come," Bec panted, tits bouncing, her dark skin glistening with sweat. "Fuck, Van, I'm close."

"Do it. I wanna hear you scream."

Savannah toyed with Bec's clit now, rubbing her thumb along the swollen flesh. Hearing her soft cries as she strained for release turned her on.

"I'm so . . . oh, *Van* . . ."

"Harder!"

She watched as Bec writhed, eyes closed,

mouth parted in ecstasy. When she froze, suspended above her in bliss, Savannah absorbed the sound of her orgasm, as if it were her own.

Like a flash of lightning, Savannah's desire pierced through her, and all she could think about was coming with them both inside her.

"Faster, Arcas," she ordered, tapping at her clit as Bec continued to pummel her ass.

His tongue lazily lapped at her nipple, tracing patterns over her skin, building her need until she was consumed by every nuzzle, every lick. Savannah was mesmerized; she yearned to come but didn't want to break the spell.

"Or what?" he echoed, the previous taunt piercing through the haze. "Will you punish me?"

"Fuck!"

"Does Emmaline like to be punished, too?"

Savannah panted, unable to control herself.

"Does the Duke finger her through her heavy skirts until she's nice and wet?"

"Oh."

"Does he bend her over and fuck her until she obeys?"

"Arcas!"

"Or is she a wanton bitch, who loves nothing more than to spread her legs?"

"*Please.*"

"Just." Thrust. "Like." Lick. "You." Bite.

Savannah succumbed to the carousel of images that played in her mind, aroused by his suggestions. The pressure in her ass and pussy, the tingling in her clit, all threw her over the edge, and she shattered into a million pieces. Body jerking, she came, unable to fight the building need. At the peak of her orgasm, she squirted, drenching Arcas' hand and the dildos inside her.

Savannah's heart pounded and she lay on the mattress, breathless and slightly stunned. Images of their threesome flashed in her mind. She had been fucked and fulfilled and every part of her body throbbed in satisfaction.

When she was able to move, she drew Arcas' hand to her mouth once again then watched as his eyes glazed over. Oh yes, he was beyond aroused and trembling with his own need to come.

She left the dildos inside her a little longer, relishing in the fullness. When Bec withdrew, she felt the absence keenly.

Arcas lay back as she licked and nibbled his fingers, teasing him until he called her name.

"This is your punishment." Savannah grinned. She nipped at his thumb, small, sharp bites, thrilled at his response.

Bec straddled him now, rubbing her body against his solid chest, muscles flexing as she ground herself over him.

Savannah sucked on his finger, turned on by the sight of him kissing another woman. His breathing became shallow, discordant. She knew he was close but continued to toy with him, knowing it would arouse him further.

Taking her time, she sucked on his thumb once more, watching as Bec rubbed her pussy along his torso, inserting the index finger of Arcas' other hand in her mouth.

When Bec came, a sharp, sudden cry, she knew he wasn't far off. A woman's orgasm always drove him wild.

And then it happened. A sudden rushing, a jolt of his torso. Arcas stiffened and cursed.

Calling her name, eyes closed in pleasure, he came.

Chapter Five

I t was on her break at the library café a few days later when she logged on to her new website.

Savannah shifted in her seat, playing with the sliced eggplant peeking out of her grilled vegetable panini. Where to start? She licked her finger, savoring the creamy pesto when she thought of her blog title.

Sexcapades: My Sex Challenge.

She looked at the blank screen, running the pads of her fingers over the keyboard, blocking out the chatter of small children and workers on their lunch break.

Recalling the threesome with Bec and Arcas on the weekend, she knew she would need a rating system. That way she would know which sexual experience tickled her fancy and what made it so tantalizing.

She began:

Ida Brady

Sexcapades - Double Your Pleasure

I love the feeling of being filled. You know what I'm talking about. That sensation like you couldn't fit anything else in any more orifices or you'd die of pleasure. I'm talking about DP, peeps. That double penetration that makes the yearning, aching feeling disappear.

While I've seen a lot of it online, I'd never tried it before. Now I don't know why the hell I waited so long, because it was ahh-mazing.

Perhaps it was watching the other woman fuck me in the ass while my boyfriend banged my pussy with a dildo or watching her tits bounce as she found her own pleasure. I know having multiple hands on my body drove me wild.

A little backdoor and kitty cat action, and I'm gagging for more. It doesn't matter what device goes where, as it's aaaaall good.

Beginning with a butt plug was a nice way to ease back into anal. Add some clit stimulation and the heavy weight of your man on top, and it's all stations to O town. Oh! And not to mention nipple clamps . . . Where have you been all my life?

I'm going to need a bigger sex box for my new toys after this year is over. Gotta say, it's a solid 9/10 on the O-meter.

Yours,

The Gamer's Girlfriend

The signature popped into her head, and she found it a fitting moniker. She *was* a gamer's girlfriend, after all.

Savannah grinned at her laptop screen, a giddy thrill suffusing through her. It felt right. Good. Like finally mastering a foreign language, it all made sense.

Let the Sexcapades begin.

Chapter Six

E mmaline closed the door to her sister's room. Anne had taken ill at their picnic and much to her surprise, the Duke had provided one of his own rooms on the estate for her respite. Emmaline was determined to accompany Anne back to her aunt's home, not three miles hence, but His Grace had insisted upon allowing her a chance to regain her health.

Emmaline had been suspicious of his intentions. Their previous interaction still weighed on her mind. She recalled the manner in which his green eyes had darkened, how he had caught her in such a compromising position.

Her cheeks heated. She hoped it was not that. She hoped it had been Anne's suitor, Lord Fanworth, ever attentive and kind, that had convinced his friend to act in such a charitable fashion. Still, Anne had yet to secure a proposal from Fanworth, and until that happy event occurred, she would be wise to be on her guard.

But now she was a guest of the Duke, invited to dine with his party. She was out of place. A spinster, a poor one, living only on the edges of polite society. Except she was here, at the behest of His Grace, no doubt due to her aunt's, the Duchess of Carrington's influence.

She trembled at the memory of his eyes on her naked flesh. The wanton way she had exposed herself.

Emmaline pressed her hand upon her cheek. She felt fevered and could only hope she was not afflicted as her sister, as she doubted she would receive the same tender care. His Grace could not be capable of that much good will.

Frowning, Emmaline cast her eye down the hall leading away from the room her sister had been given. She reached the landing and turned in the opposite direction, in search of the rest of the party.

Again, she was overwhelmed by the size and beauty of his home. Every inch of it gleamed. It spoke of a history of wealth that dated back generations.

Emmaline adjusted her posture, undaunted. She would not be cowed. She may be a poor gentleman's daughter, but even the most discerning eye could not fault her appearance.

Wandering now in admiration, she peeked in each room she passed. A number were clearly unused: a guest bedroom, a lady's boudoir. Some were *still decorated in the older style, with wood paneling and heavy furniture. In one room, she was overwhelmed by the green and brown furnishings. Very masculine and stately. She dared to wander farther in, looking around her in admiration.*

She did not see the door to the adjoining room or that it was open until she was upon him, His Grace, standing before a looking glass.

Emmaline gasped. The Duke straightened and met her gaze in the mirror. His expression was grim. The button of his shirt was undone, so that a hard column of throat was revealed. She was drawn to that triangle of skin, caught by a need that flared bright and quick at the sight.

They stood, gazing at each other in the mirror, chests rising.

The Duke's green eyes, dark pools of disdain, now heated and focused entirely on her.

Her color was up; she could feel the warmth spread across her cheeks and down her bosom. What was this sensation? Loathing, surely. But there was a discomfort beneath it, an awareness of him as a man.

One with whom she was alone. Unchaperoned.

Her aunt would send out a search party if she lingered.

"I suppose it is only fitting that you see me naked. I believe it makes us even, would you not agree, Miss Collins?"

His haughty, smug manner irked her. She would

not allow him to belittle her. She cared not for what had passed between them. Or for the manner in which he had stared at the place between her thighs with . . .

Emmaline's chest heaved, her stays unbearably tight.

Hunger. He had looked upon her in a greedy, covetous manner. It had accompanied her through the lonely nights since, teasing her body, tormenting her mind until she could no longer ignore the sensation.

Emmaline turned on her heel.

"Wait."

And froze.

Drawing in a deep breath, evoking the courage of an admiral at war, Emmaline faced him.

"Yes, Your Grace?"

The Duke of Maddern's movements were stiff, his tone formal. "I wish to inquire after the health of your sister."

His question appeared to come from an honorable place. Emmaline was shocked.

His manner of speaking was not fit for such an intimate space. Eager for their conversation to end, Emmaline leveled her voice, channeling her sister's patience and kindness. In truth, she wanted nothing more than to smite him soundly.

"Fine. I thank you."

"Does she require any further care?"

"No."

"Did the physician make any suggestions to her comfort?"

Emmaline glared. "If you are insinuating that we move her, I have it on good authority that she is not to be disturbed for the next four and twenty hours. She is weak and poorly. I apologize for any discomfort we may cause by invading your privacy, and I wish it were not the case. Trust me when I say, Your Grace, that I would rather not be standing here conversing with you."

"I dare say you had other ideas in mind."

Emmaline's mouth opened. She did not care if her accompanying snort was not ladylike. "I should think a gentleman would not remind a, a . . ." She fumbled for the word. No lady would be here, in a man's dressing room, conversing with him unchaperoned. No lady would— "I should think a gentleman would not have referenced . . . that previous incident."

"Ah. Your little interlude in the greenhouse—" He stepped closer. "I would apologize for intruding, except to say, I enjoyed it."

Emmaline's hand flew to her mouth. The trembling began in her chest anew, fanning out across her extremities.

"I was merely inquiring about the health of your sister." Yet his green eyes evoked something far more carnal. The Duke pressed closer.

"Do not toy with me." Emmaline could not place her anger, uncertain of why it bubbled beneath her skin. Her good sense had abandoned her the minute he had approached.

His Grace eliminated the distance between them. Emmaline retreated. The hard panels of the wall reminded her she was trapped, not that she feared him. It was her trembling heart that left her breathless.

He came closer still.

"You provoke me. In truth, I cannot stop picturing you in the greenhouse. Your legs parted, your soft flesh bared to me."

Emmaline swallowed then regretted it. He had pinned her to the wall with his gaze alone.

Who knew his shoulders could block out the light? They were broad and manly. The pulse at the base of his neck beat strong and steadily.

He flicked a heavy glance at the swell of her breasts. The cut of her gown was a bolder fashion than any dress she owned. Her nipples hardened, their sensitive peaks seeking his attention. She should flee.

"Miss Collins?"

"I have nothing to say, Your Grace."

"Perhaps you are more comfortable with doing."

The Duke leaned in, resting his forearm on the panel above her head. His voice, when it came, was gravelly and rough, thick with desire. "Tell me, Miss Collins, did you think of me that afternoon? Did you picture me joining you, burying myself in your—"

"Your Grace!"

"*Perhaps if I touched you, just here.*" His hand hovered, a whisper, between her thighs. "*You might be more responsive?*"

"*You are taking liberties of which you have no right.*" She cleared her throat, scarcely able to draw breath. *If he would but move a fraction, she would be free of him.*

The Duke grinned, his eyes two burning emeralds. "*I am a duke, if you have forgotten. And of late, a careless one. The image of you naked has begun to elicit a particularly . . . sinful reaction in me.*"

Emmaline's breathing was shallow. She did not wish to make contact. She refused to succumb to his wicked seduction.

"*You are seeking a response, Your Grace. One which I refuse to give.*"

"*Yet.*" His voice tickled her ear. He shifted, standing tall.

Now was her chance to leave.

Emmaline gasped when a pair of strong arms gripped her waist, drawing her flush against his hard chest.

"*Merciful heavens!*" she cried out, all propriety lost.

"*Your impertinence . . . It is maddening. Arousing. Do you know how many nights I have thought about you, legs splayed, fingers buried in your wet folds? You were ripe and ready for plucking that day.*" His eyes burned; his voice beckoned.

"*I—I shall scream,*" she answered in response.

The deep rumble in his chest mocked her resolve.

Dash it, why did she sound so very weak? Yes, she hated the man who loomed before her, but in truth, she was painfully affected by him. This was carnal desire. For the Duke of Maddern, of all men. It was insufferable. Astonishing.

And yet . . .

Emmaline closed the gap, unaware that in one breath she had betrayed herself, but she was drowning. Drowning under the thick, heavy current of desire, in which Duke was the sea, drawing her in until her feet were no longer on solid ground.

His mouth was hard, his passion demanding. At a loss, she clung to him. It was glorious and dangerous. Thrilling and painful.

She yearned for more.

Her breasts crushed against the hard planes of his body as he wrapped his arms around her.

Emmaline mimicked his strokes, eager to taste him, emboldened by the kiss. It was wanton, but she cared not of the consequences when in his arms.

His Grace groaned. The low, deep sound reverberated through her dress, dancing across her naked flesh beneath.

Raking her fingers through his thick, dark hair and down the naked column at his throat, Emmaline allowed him to guide her. She followed his lead, succumbing to his mastery until the stirring began, deep in her womb. What was this thrilling need that anchored her to him? How could it be that His Grace was the man to elicit it?

His hands trailed down her back, stoking the fire. When he cupped her bottom and squeezed, she moaned against his mouth, shock and arousal fighting for purchase.

Momentarily, the Duke drew back, pressing her body against the wall. He trailed feverish kisses across her cheek and down her neck.

"You are sweeter than nectar. But like the bee's sting, you pain me."

His tongue traced the swell of her breasts. His hot breath followed. Emmaline writhed against him, agitated. The building, climbing sensation began.

"Pain you?" She cupped his head as he feasted on the sensitive curve of her neck, overwhelmed. She felt his mouth curve along the column of her throat.

The Duke pressed his hips against her belly.

Emmaline's eyes flew open.

"This is what you do to me," he breathed. "This arousal keeps me up at night."

Emmaline searched for a response, in vain.

"At a loss for words? I am astonished."

She grew hot with awareness. Slowly, reason filtered through the haze that surrounded them. What in heavens had she done, allowing him to take such liberties?

His valet could interrupt them at any moment.

Maddern lowered his head, his kiss now gentle, a caress. It surprised her, to learn he was capable of such tenderness. He cradled her face, stroking the side of her cheek while taking her raging desire down to a simmering burn.

How many times had she dreamed of his kisses as a young girl? How many days had she spent hoping he would claim her as his duchess?

Oh yes, he affected her, but Emmaline had lived content for many years without his touch. She would be able to find that peace once more.

She broke away, vision cloudy.

The Duke stepped back once, then again until they were almost at an acceptable distance.

"I did not mean to startle you, Miss Collins. In fact, I must apologize." His voice was stiff, as if the words had been disused for a century. "I hope I have not offended you."

"Offe . . .?" She pressed a hand to her mouth. She dared not reveal the truth to him, fearful that he would take advantage again. She shifted away from the wall and towards the open door, seeking distance.

She would find some refreshments for her sister. And pray she received a good dose of common sense for herself along the way.

Maddern's eyebrows rose. An infuriatingly smug smile tilted his lips. Curse that man.

"You need not tell a lie on my account."

"Your Grace, if this little display of licentious-ness says anything, it was that you are a wicked, underhanded rake. A gentleman would never take advantage of their guest."

"It was you that interrupted me. And may I remind you, you proved to be more than eager for the advantage moments before."

"I beg your pardon! How dare you speak to me in such a manner?"

"How dare I?" Maddern's eyes flashed. "Your bosom betrays you, Miss Collins. If I so wish it, you would find yourself naked and very much willing beneath me."

Emmaline was distraught. Tears threatened. This would not do. He was a duke, a powerful, wealthy peer, able to do as he wished with whomever he chose. She was merely a diversion. She would never be anything meaningful to him.

She would do well to steer clear of his presence from here on.

"I would beseech you to keep a gentleman's honor about this, Your Grace. That this shall never happen again."

"If this is as you wish?"

"I wish it with all my heart."

Chapter Seven

"Which nineteenth-century hero are you fucking tonight?" Arcas' voice was dripping with sarcasm.

Savannah opened her eyes. Her fingers were in the waistband of her panties, which were soaked thanks to Maddern and his commanding presence.

She hadn't heard Arcas come in, not that that meant anything. She couldn't hear anything except the heated exchange between Maddern and Emmaline; the blood rushing in her ears blocked out the rest.

Arcas stopped beside the bed. He flicked the book closed, glancing at the cover. "*Love and Honor*? Again?"

"I needed a classic."

"What you need is new material and a good fuck."

"Are you offering?"

In seconds, her shorts and panties were flung across the room, with her feet braced against the back of his wheelchair. His hot breath hovered at her ankles before he yanked her closer.

"Did Maddern fuck Emmaline like this?"

His tongue swirled patterns on the inside of her thighs. Like a match, she ignited on the first strike.

Savannah groaned. Experience told her that when he face fucked her, she would come in long, luxurious waves. He was able to build her arousal with his tongue, keeping her on edge for what felt like hours.

She didn't know what was hotter: his mouth or the fact that he knew most of the books she read nearly as well as she did.

The soft, slow rhythmic licking at her clit was deliberate. He knew she was close and still, he chose to tease her. Perhaps he had more in common with Maddern that she thought.

"More."

"Does Emmaline beg?" Arcas murmured.

Savannah looked up into a pair of wicked green eyes. Yes, he was aroused too. She had seen that look many times, and it never failed to set her alight.

"No."

"But you will."

"Please . . ."

"I can't hear you."

"*Arcas*. Fuck me."

His grin was smug, appreciative. And when his

tongue thrust into her, she cried out. Savannah's hips jerked, her laugh incredulous. She was getting what she wanted, even if she squirmed beneath the weight of his arms on her waist, keeping her still.

And then he fucked her, driving in and out, sending her a little wilder, a little wetter with every stroke. He flicked his thumb over her clit, and the pressure was everything she had been craving.

She was already quivering, wet with need from the Duke's attentions to Emmaline. She wasn't going to last long with Arcas' expert hands and mouth on her now. His tongue was thick, his fingers soft, and the image of his face buried in her wet snatch was all that she needed to come.

Gasping, unable and unwilling to stop herself, Savannah let go. Her legs were trembling, her breathing ragged, the peak just as sudden and glorious as she expected. She rocked against him, wanting to savor every second.

When Arcas drew back, she sat up, ready to return the pleasure. She was stopped by the sound of his alarm.

"No time for a bit of fun?"

"Another raid. This was just a short break."

"You can raid me again, if you like?"

Arcas grinned, his smile boyish. She enjoyed watching him. He was intense yet sweet, loyal but up for a good time. Desire stirred inside her just looking at his lips, knowing that he would be wearing her scent in his next raid.

She shifted off the bed, straddling him in the wheelchair, rubbing her breasts against his chest. He gripped her ass, kneading her, arousing her all over again.

Arcas shifted aside her silk top, pausing to stroke and tease her nipples before raking his nails down her stomach. Savannah leaned back and watched him toy with her snatch, tracing her labia, pink and swollen from his mouth. He worked his fingers in and out now, fucking her with one hand, tweaking her heavy breast with the other. All the while, she gripped the sides of his wheelchair, shuddering and jerking. Desperate to come again.

"More."

"You like it thick, don't you?"

"*More*, I said."

"Is that an order, Van?"

"I wanna come on your fingers."

"Really?"

She pouted at him, moaning.

"And do you think about me fucking you like the Duke of Maddern?"

Her breath hitched, the very idea of it more of a turn-on than she had expected. They both knew it was an impossibility. But still . . . he knew she loved nothing more than dirty talk.

"Yes."

"You know I'm thick, and long, and so fucking hard."

"I want it. I want you."

"I'd bend you over that table, lifting your heavy dress. Your breasts would spill out onto the cold surface, and I'd take out my cock, rubbing it against your snatch."

Arcas inserted a fourth finger and with the other hand, pressed down on her abdomen. The dizzying pressure, the swirling, clawing need intensified, and when he inched forward to suck on her exposed nipple, Savannah swore.

"Then?" she panted.

Arcas feasted on her breasts, biting and sucking while his fingers flew out of her pussy. She rode his hand, watching his tongue licking her tits, reveling in the sound of him pounding into her.

A notification pinged in the distance.

"Faster," she urged, bouncing on him, the rocking motion catapulting her closer to her orgasm. With every thrust, she grew wetter, hotter, hungrier.

"Then I'd spread that wet pussy and pound into you, slapping that ass, watching it jiggle."

"Arcas, I'm . . ."

Images. Sinful, sexy images of Arcas dressed like Maddern, fucking her in a library was all too much. She succumbed to the fantasy, to the tantalizing pleasure of his fingers fucking her. The buildup was glorious, but she was unable to control herself, climbing to the peak with greedy, eager thrusts.

And then she fell, diving deep in the vortex of her need, relishing in her own pulsing, throbbing release. Spinning out of control, she landed in a heap against his chest, her body flushed and sated.

"Well done, Emmaline."

Savannah wrapped her arms around his neck, laughing, breathless. "You know what I like."

Arcas kissed her under her ear, at the valley where her jaw met her neck. "Gotta keep my woman happy."

"Always. But desire is a two-way street."

"I thought it was the name of that streetcar," he mimicked.

"You know, for a gamer, you're very well read."

"Not just a pretty face." He bit her shoulder then shifted to look at her. "You can devour me later."

"I intend to."

He lifted her off his lap, tumbling her onto the bed.

Savannah squealed, laughing. "Enjoy your raid."

"Feel free to come and party any time."

"Tempting, but the Duke calls. Maybe to-morrow night?"

"Done." Arcas grinned, wheeling out of the room and into his own world of fantasy.

Chapter Eight

Sexcapades - BDSMmm

While every girl loves nothing more than watching her boyfriend suck on her tits, there's something very erotic about being tied up and blindfolded when engaging in a BDSM bonk in the bedroom. Not knowing when my boyfriend's teeth were about to graze my nipples was a lesson in restraint. But it was delicious as much as torturous.

The soft leather of the whip turning into a sharp sting on my bare flesh, the sounds of the paddle whistling through the air before landing on my ass . . . it's all enhanced when you can't see a damn thing.

Not that I found it a hindrance. If anything, my lack of sight was an even greater turn-on. Everything was heightened, as if my body became hyper-sensitive to even the slightest shift or sigh.

So by the time he fucked me, I was aroused beyond

belief. And begging. Yes, positively begging for him to make me come.

Full disclosure, the ball gag was uncomfortable, and a little suffocating for my liking. But I guess you don't know your triggers until you're sobbing into your boyfriend's shoulder.

I'm learning what I'm comfortable with, in the mind and the flesh. I'm learning my boundaries and have decided I'll try everything, at least once.

But what I loved about being blindfolded was the element of anticipation. Would the next stroke be hard or soft? Fast or slow? Everything is bound by the senses, every nerve in my body alert.

If I touched my clit, I was punished. If I made a sound, I was punished. And the punishment came often and in the form of absence. No dildo in my pussy. No fingering of my clit. Nothing but his breath on my body and the warmth of his chest hovering above me, ever so out of reach. I have lovely little reminders of my impatience on my wrists.

But the naughtiest punishment was the ice in my ass . . . I'm a very naughty sub, after all.

I'd like to try it again, perhaps with chains instead of leather next time.

A 7/10 on the O-meter.

Yours,

The Gamer's Girlfriend.

Savannah was in the mood for an adventure. After a busy week and more shifts than she thought humanly possible, she was up for some gaming escapism.

She logged on, choosing her avatar, one that was a healer in the form of a fairy-human. She admired her avatar's long glistening wings. The figure was unnaturally lean to have breasts that large, but she had given up thinking about true representations in gaming a long time ago.

Savannah had no energy to get annoyed about it either. It had been a long day, and she just wanted oblivion. She had skipped the post-work drinks and opted for curling up beside Arcas for a bit of computer action . . . and hopefully a bit more if she was lucky. From the look in his eyes when she'd walked in, she'd say she was going to score.

Savannah contemplated changing into one of the lacy slips he had bought for her birthday but thought her black-on-black bartending clothes had caught his eye well enough. She had undone another button before she walked in the door, just so she could see his eyes glaze over. The pearl thigh chain she wore added a bit of bling to the outfit.

Savannah crossed her legs, skirt riding up her thighs. She continued to make her selections, grinning when Arcas cleared his throat.

"I know what you're doing, you little vixen."

Savannah was all innocence. *"Moi?* I have no idea what you mean. I need to focus if we want to beat these bosses, you know. I'm a healer, a very important person in this team, in case you've forgotten." Her lips curved. She couldn't lie to save her life.

Arcas' voice hummed in her ear, low and level. "I'm up for all sorts of raids tonight, sweetheart."

The delectable shiver trickled down her neck, a promise of pleasure to come. Savannah faced him now, mouth parted.

Arcas traced his finger along her lips, groaning when she bit down. "If you think I'm going to kiss you, you're mistaken. Two can play this game, Van."

She did. And was simultaneously disappointed and aroused at his control.

"Game on, Cas."

He grinned, turning away to face the screen.

"Dragon again?"

"I can't resist."

To say he loved dragons was an understatement. The man was as obsessed with them as she was with Regency romance novels. Together, they made the perfect pair.

Savannah could hear the other gamers coming online, chatting about their day. Arcas had gamed with them for a good year now, and each player was skilled and determined to progress as far as possible.

Given their skill, she wasn't certain she would be more than a mild hindrance in joining in tonight. But screw it, she liked playing. More to the point, she liked playing with Arcas.

The man knew how to fuck shit up. Those hands were quick, his mind sharp, and watching his strategy—no matter what kind of game they were playing—never failed to impress.

Focusing on the computer screen, she wiggled her chair closer to him. His job as an analyst coupled with the money he raked in as a gamer meant that all the equipment was high-end. Which meant gaming was a hell of a lot more enjoyable than she had expected.

"Ready?" He picked up his headphones.

"Let's do this."

While they were waiting for the rest of the guild to join, Savannah spoke to the others about her shifts at the library and the new bar that had opened a few blocks away, before Arcas made the call to begin.

For the next forty minutes, they cleared up to the boss. Savannah, while a little rusty, quickly got into the groove.

Before they entered the castle dungeon, they paused to go through tactics. Arcas discussed their positions and ran through the main mechanics, ensuring everyone knew their roles.

"Van will heal me, and don't stand in the fire."

There was a titter of laughter amongst the group.

Arcas counted them down, and that brief suspension of time, the build-up before they charged in, never failed to thrill her.

The demon stood waiting in the middle of the room, chest heaving, purple wings outspread. His torso was large, his chest bare and imposing as he towered over them all. Briefly, Savannah wondered what it would be like to be fucked by a demon, but no sooner had the thought entered her mind than it dissipated; she became immersed in the game, watchful of the damage dealers.

Savannah stood back as Arcas and the other tank, Slayer, led the raid. She focused on healing Arcas, until the tanks switched.

When the acid spilled on the floor, Van jumped out of the way but quickly recovered her concentration on Slayer.

"This guy hits hard," Slayer muttered, his voice, deep and accented, sliding through the speakers.

"Don't die, motherfucker," Savannah teased.

Five minutes later, their first boss defeated, Arcas and Savannah had a rhythm, and after two hours, they had progressed considerably.

"I thought I would bring this along to increase the stakes," Arcas murmured, his microphone switched off as they took a five-minute break.

Savannah glanced at what he was holding and smirked. "You're just as dirty as I am."

"I think it's time we turned up the heat."

"You just want to watch me squirm."

"Can't say that isn't a side bonus."

"You know we're about to start on the next wing soon, right?"

"My timing, Van, is never an issue."

Savannah glanced over, taking the vibrator from his hands, but it wouldn't budge.

"I'll do the honors."

She stood in front of him, lifting her skirt so that he missed nothing. She slipped off her panties, bending at the waist to pick them up, her ass and pussy spread for his viewing pleasure.

Arcas' laughter was low, filled with appreciation. "Best view I've had all night."

She sat on his lap, back against his chest.

"I don't know what you mean."

His mouth was close to her ear, issuing out instructions. "Sure you don't. Spread your legs now, minx."

Grinning, Savannah leaned against his chest and flicked her legs out in a V.

Arcas turned on the device and trailed it up the inside of her thigh, brushing along her clit, circling her in slow, deliberate movements until she shivered.

"Are you going to just tease me, or will you use that thing?"

He shook his head at her impatience. "Haven't you ever heard that all good things come to those who wait?"

"That's said by boring people. I want it all now."

"Naughty, naughty."

He toyed with her clit, running the vibrator up

and down, and around in circles until she was arching against him, moaning loudly.

Savannah wanted to fuck, she was impatient for it, but Arcas liked to be in charge.

He pinched her breasts through the fabric of her shirt and she almost lost control. She was a live wire of energy, desperate for a charge.

When he inserted the device inside her, she almost fell off his lap. She was so aroused, so desperate for more, it was painful to wait.

"I don't think I'm going to last," she panted.

"How about we give them something to talk about?" Arcas murmured against her cheek.

Through her dazed state, Savannah grinned. "A little voyeur action?"

"The sound of you coming is better than any raid. Might be something nice for you to write about."

"Ever the altruist." Her breath hitched in her throat. He knew of new ways to arouse her, to drive her closer to orgasm, closer to the next high.

"Do it," she muttered. The thrill of it shot up her body, expectation brushing along her skin.

Arcas flicked on his microphone. "I'm back." He spoke to the four other members of the party.

"Where's Van?"

"Ohhh." She could barely see, let alone raid.

"She's here."

Suddenly there was silence.

Savannah's breathing quickened as the pulsing

Virtue

sensation of the vibrator did its work. She gyrated her hips, panting loudly, turned on by the people listening. It was bold and daring, and utterly arousing.

Arcas was praising her, whispering words of encouragement.

"Yes!"

She heard one of the men swear. "Is she . . ."

"Give us a second here. I think my girl is close."

"What is she wearing?" asked another.

"Mmm," Savannah groaned. She was teetering between being lost in the radiating waves of pleasure and the awareness of strangers on the chat. She pictured them at their screens, slipping their hands down their pants, palming their cocks, stroking their cunts as they got off listening to her. It was fucking hot.

"A short skirt. Thigh chain. No panties. Her legs splayed while she gets fucked by a vibrator."

"Can we see?"

The thought of other men and women watching her come suddenly sent her body into hyperdrive.

Arcas squeezed her tits, increasing the vibrations as he pounded her. He continued stroking her clit in the steady rhythmic way that made her lose her mind. Savannah didn't hold back.

"Fuck!" she cried out, hips bucking and gyrating.

"Too late," Arcas muttered.

The force exploded through her body, sudden

and powerful. Savannah's legs shook, her body twitched, reeling from the onslaught. She gripped his hand, trembling now at the throbbing in her pussy.

Savannah drew in a ragged breath, then another, heart dancing to a discordant beat. In a daze, she took out the vibrator then watched as Arcas licked it clean. He had unlocked a part of her sexuality that had remained dormant for so long. She would have to thank him for that later.

Savannah leaned into his microphone. "I hope you enjoyed access to this exclusive content," she murmured.

One of the girls choked. "Best. Raid. Ever."

A few hours later, Arcas pulled off the headset and pushed back from the desk.

"That was a successful raid."

Savannah stretched. "Which one?"

"I was talking about the game. But I did enjoy our show. From the sounds of it, you did too."

"I did. It's another first for me, so I have you to thank for that."

"We'll have to put that on repeat. Another entry for your Sexcapades?"

"Mhmm. You know me—"

"Up for anything."

Savannah winked, moving closer. "Clever man."

She picked up his hand and began to massage his palm, working her way down the length of each digit, paying special attention to the joints.

He licked his lips, mouth parting; she could tell he was eager for more, but he remained patient, watchful. He always had a strength of resolve she could never muster. He ate his chocolate in small nibbles, where she would break off large chunks. His ice cream was savored with long licks, where she would bite and devour.

And when he fucked her . . . it was a glorious feast, an indulgence of mind and body that suspended her in an agonizing state of arousal for hours.

Savannah stroked up each finger, then slowly down again, but it was his thumb that elicited the most electric of responses. She circled the tip of it then caressed the length, taking her time, teasing him gently.

When he had told her about the erogenous zones in his fingers, Savannah had been intrigued. When she had seen his response, she wanted more. It was arousing to love him this way, to know that he experienced an intense pleasure, his own powerful orgasm in this manner. Savannah noticed the pulse at the base of his neck, throbbing in expectation.

She leaned closer, nipping the tip of his thumb with her teeth. Arcas gasped, muttering her name.

She used her mouth now, rubbing her lips along his length then taking him in. She swirled his thumb with her tongue, stroking and sucking until his torso tensed. She brought him to the edge, then backed off. Over and over, she toyed with him until he was panting and growling at her to finish.

His dark hair fell across his face; his eyes were impossibly bright.

"You're a witch."

"A fairy actually." She smirked. "I just thought, seeing as though you're all about delayed gratification, that you might want to hold off a little."

"Funny."

"I thought so."

Savannah continued, increasing the pressure, alternating between nips and licks. His hand grabbed the back of her head, fingers twisting in her hair. He was lost in his own pleasure, and she took her time, starting and stopping, building his desire until he groaned her name. She sucked him hard, maintaining a steady pressure.

"Van," he murmured. His torso jerked, his head fell back, and the sight set off her own need once again. Arcas' orgasm looked intense, as if it radiated through his body, shocking his system.

But when those green eyes turned to her, heating in appreciation, she shivered.

"I'm not done yet," he muttered, dragging her up.

He kissed her in greedy bites, running his

hands along her sides, teasing her with those clever fingers. Her body vibrated. She stripped him of his T-shirt, marveling at the sculpted muscle, then whipped her own clothes over her head, discarding her bra in quick, hurried movements. She wanted to feel his chest against her own. She craved contact, knowing the friction would send her wild.

Savannah ran a finger down one pec and then the other.

The contrast of his muscle and her soft flesh sent fresh waves of lust through her body. But it was his heavy, hungry gaze lingering over her breasts and hips that left a warm glow in her heart.

Yes, she needed to come. Yes, she wanted to fuck. But not just anyone. It had to be him. The way he looked at her, touched her, wanted her, surpassed anything she had experienced before. Because it was him, only him, that could captivate her body and soul.

She reveled in the heavy, delicious ache that trailed from her abdomen down to her pussy. She continued the slow, sensual torture, brushing her breasts against his chest, shuddering when her nipples pebbled.

Arcas palmed her ass, kneading and squeezing, driving her yet again to the point where desire clouded her mind, where she had no other outlet but to fuck.

His fingers circled her clit then dipped inside

her. He repeated the move over and over, the soft, slick sound penetrating the silence, turning her on.

"What do you want me to do?"

"Touch me."

"Where?" He nibbled against her neck.

"Everywhere," she gasped, rocking her hips, needing to be filled.

Arcas bit down on her shoulder, and she yelped in shock.

He ran his hands down her arms, brushing the sides of her breasts but never fully touching. The man was the ultimate conductor. He knew how to play her, to draw out her notes, tapping and plucking until she sang. Savannah's sighs filled the space around them.

It was maddening.

Arcas drew invisible patterns on her hip, that small section of skin that she found overwhelming to touch. But he did, slowly, relentlessly, until she was pitching back and forth, pleading with him to take her.

When those fingers found her clit, she sobbed.

"Yes." Savannah grabbed his hair, fisting it when he guided her up. He sucked and licked her breasts, a fire and frenzy burning out of control.

And his fingers, those long, strong, thick fingers plundered.

"Don't stop!" she called out, eager.

And so he gave, more friction, more fingers, stretching her, filling her, while his thumb worked over her clit. She was dizzy, falling, captured and yet somehow free.

The rippling of her orgasm began, and Savannah groaned, low and long, succumbing to it with abandon. She was weightless and yet heavy, bound to this pleasure. To him. As the orgasm built, stealing her breath, Savannah let go, riding Arcas and her desire until there was nothing left to give.

This was what he did to her, filling her yet hollowing her out, so that she was often spent and shaken once they had sex. It was his intensity that she craved, in every aspect of their lives.

Savannah placed a dizzying kiss on his lips, knowing there would be more to come once they got to bed.

He looked like a man half-starved, so she would let him feast.

Chapter Nine

Savannah curled up on the couch, allowing the tears to fall.

What the hell were her parents doing at the restaurant? Had they deliberately sought her out? Had her siblings let slip about where she worked?

It had been a shock to see them. Almost as shocking as when they had caught her with a boy in her college dorm. She had received a lecture of almighty proportions that day, then texts from her older brother, imploring her to change her ways. Piers was the good Christian boy they had raised, the man of the house should anything happen to their father.

When her phone had pinged upon returning home, she had cursed herself for not buying a new sim.

You're living a life of sin.

> You need to turn to God and repent of your ways.

> The Lord loves you, Savannah. Let Jesus in. He can heal all wounds. He can forgive your mistakes.

> Please, don't tear this family apart with your sin.

> God loves you, even if you don't love yourself.

Savannah had sent an SOS to Arcas then turned off her phone. Her stomach churned, as she knew it would be filled with fifty messages from her brother attempting to bring her back into the fold.

It would be comical if it weren't so damn upsetting.

For as long as she could remember, she was never good enough, never clean enough, never Christian enough for her family. Every step was one of trepidation, of knowing that everything she did was wrong. The shame had been an oppressive weight, so much that it was still difficult to discard those feelings even years later.

She had been shamed and punished for so long, she had initially found it difficult to know what was normal and what wasn't.

Some memories were better left buried.

But every family had to have one black sheep. And she had been the scapegoat, happy to submit to their abuse if it meant her siblings didn't suffer.

When they tried to force her into an arranged marriage, she knew she had to leave. It was a good thing she had developed a backbone in college, otherwise she would have given in to their demands tonight. She was ashamed to admit it had been tempting as a broke college student to crave what was familiar, even if it was destructive. But over time, that feeling had passed. She loved herself too much to go back there, to feel second-rate, inferior, damaged.

They just couldn't accept that she was a sexually active twenty-four-year-old who didn't want to be a part of the church or—shock horror—have babies.

She was happy exploring her sexuality without the condemnation of burning in hell looming over her shoulder.

But it still hurt.

The people who were meant to love her the most, ended up hurting her worse than any ex-boyfriend had, or would.

Savannah pressed her knuckles into her swollen eyes. They would be puffy and sunken in the morning, but she didn't care. She'd have to explain to her friends what had happened, and no doubt, the tears would come.

When she heard the apartment door close a few minutes later, she relaxed into the cushion, the tension in her shoulders dissipating a fraction.

Arcas was home.

"I got your text."

And the fresh waves of tears fell. She sobbed even as he lifted her, cradling her in his lap.

"It's okay. I'm here. Let it out, Van."

She nestled into his arms, thankful to have someone in her life who accepted her, loved her, without wanting to change her.

Arcas wheeled her to their bedroom. After a while, she crawled onto the bed and waited until he lay down beside her before she began.

"They came to the restaurant. The more I think about it, the more I think it was deliberate."

"How did they know?"

"Gail must have let it slip. She was questioning the church and talking about leaving. So I let her know where I worked in case she needed to find me . . . Sounds like they changed her mind for her." She remembered the way her sister had sobbed over the phone, saying she never wanted to go back home, that she was going to run away. Savannah had calmed her down enough to convince her to have a plan, to do it right, or she'd end up relying on them again. She thought the next time she spoke to her would be to welcome her to her new life.

"Fucking bastards need to get a grip."

Savannah swallowed, tongue heavy, mouth dry.

Arcas tucked a strand of hair behind her ear. "I'm so sorry they harassed you at work."

"They waited for me to go on my break."

"How kind."

Savannah barked out a bitter laugh, hiccupping.

"They know I'm living with you, and they think I should move back home. Oh, and apparently, I dress like a harlot."

"They said that?"

"Yes. And if I didn't believe their word, they would send the messengers from God to hold a mirror up to my soul, to follow me and teach me the error of my ways."

"Fuck, Van. That's stalking."

"They did it when I was in college, after they caught me getting head from a guy."

Arcas' mouth curved. "Was it good head?"

Savannah wanted to laugh but couldn't. In the end, she just shook her head. "It took me ages to be comfortable having a guy go down on me after that."

"Van, honey, this is all the more reason to get some kind of restraining order against them."

Savannah shrugged, immediately defensive. They were her parents. She couldn't do that to them.

"They don't seem to feel any remorse doing it to you," he cajoled, reading her mind.

She stared back at him, heart aching for what she had never had. For what she would never have from her parents. Hell, she wasn't allowed any contact with her siblings. Some of them were too young to remember her, and others were too brainwashed to know any better. She had come to the sad realization she would never be able to see most of them again.

"I'm not ready for that."

"When and if you are, you tell me and we'll go down to the station together. Van, you're not dirty; you're not sinful. What we have together isn't wrong. You're sweet and kind and fun, and you're entitled to live your life however the fuck you please. Even if you were the devil in disguise, you deserve to make your own choices coz you're an adult."

"I know. But it still hurts."

"And it makes you doubt yourself. For just a second, you begin to question your choices, and that's way too much time to give them power over you." Arcas ran his hand down her back, the slow, rhythmic strokes soothing the ache inside her heart.

She nodded, offering a small smile.

Finally, he asked, "What can I do to help?"

"This. Talking to you. It all helps."

He kissed her temple.

"Remember all of this when you wake up in the morning feeling displaced guilt. Their rules don't apply anymore."

"Why can't they love me?" Savannah sobbed, heartache blanketing any courage she had felt at his advice. "Why c-can't I be okay without their approval?"

Arcas held her close against his chest, giving her all the unspoken support she needed. Her mouth was parched, her eyes swollen, every part of her tender and bruised.

"You will be," he soothed. "This shit takes time. Trust that you're stronger than they would have you believe. Trust that I love you and care about you too much to let you go through this alone."

"Stay with me until I sleep?"

"Always."

Chapter Ten

If she could go back in time, somehow transport back to the past, Savannah would travel to nineteenth-century England. She would have to be a wealthy widow, of course. It would give her the advantage of doing as she pleased without having to worry about where the next meal was coming from; poverty for women in those times was not a romantic notion. Neither was relying on a man for one's fortune.

But aside from the realities of life in the 1800s, Savannah nevertheless found something so satisfying about occupying those worlds.

Her sexual fantasies were unwritten, secret portals into the lives of two fictional characters. The contrast between repression and desire, the boundaries and customs, made her want to be a part of that world in so many ways.

Savannah slid her hand over her breasts. She could imagine how it would feel to wear the heavy dresses and restrictive stays. The way her lover would run his hand up underneath her skirts, seeking soft flesh and an eager woman.

Savannah arched her back, racing her hands over her heated body. She could picture the exchange between William and Emmaline as if it were happening to her, as if she were Miss Collins, heated and aroused by the Duke of Maddern's kisses.

Every man who deigned to meet her would want to bed her, but she would be picky. She wouldn't fall for any handsome man, though a comely face didn't hurt. Many of the men with whom she'd had amazing sex in the past weren't the hottest guys, but they knew their way around a woman's body, and those who didn't were eager to learn.

Not that she had ever had that problem with Arcas. She had scored big time in that department.

She wondered if she was so enamored by that world because of her parents' restrictive upbringing. Born-again Christians Amy and Todd Preston had demanded their children live a life that was punishingly conservative.

Savannah had grown up surrounded by supposed miracles, ministers who were treated like rockstars, preaching to random strangers, all accompanied by an inability to live her life by her choice. A life free from deliverances and healings, free from the dogma of a religion that didn't speak to her soul.

It had taken time to feel comfortable with sex, with her identity as a woman with a high libido and a need for more than a life bound by nonsensical rules.

The bitter aftertaste from her run-in with her parents had faded over the past week, but she knew she would need to find a better way of handling their intrusions. While she knew Arcas' suggestion was a practical solution, her heart just couldn't do it. Not now at least. Perhaps one day.

A warm memory flittered past her. It was the day she had found her first Regency romance novel. She had been a teenager out with her family on a special trip to the city for a religious convention. After begging them to be allowed to browse the thrift store, she had spotted the book. The spine and cover had looked unassuming enough, but it had been the blurb, the wonderful tale of heartache and romance that had caught her imagination.

Then Savannah had done the one thing that even to this day brought her shame. She had stolen the book. Knowing she had no money, knowing her parents would burn such a novel if she asked to buy it, she had pretended to drop it then stuffed it in her satchel.

That had been her first copy of *Love and Honor*, and she had never looked back. She wouldn't look back. Not to her parents. Not to their pestering pleas or her brother's abusive texts. She was being true to herself. That was the only thing that mattered.

The funny thing was that years later, when she had run away from home so she could go to college, she'd returned to the thrift store and paid the twelve dollars for the book.

And bought another eight more.

What had started as a teenager smitten with an unfamiliar world became a much-needed source of comfort when her parents had washed their hands of her.

Would it be more thrilling back then, she wondered, to engage in something outside the marital bed? Anything that was deemed taboo would titillate the masses, so surely sex conducted in an illicit manner would have felt wonderfully naughty?

Especially if the man in question was a duke . . .

"I have a better use for that impertinent mouth," *Maddern drawled, turning to close the library door,* *locking it behind him.*

She was ruined.

How could it be that Emmaline wanted to rail at *the man before her, and yet, equally, in the same* *breath, she desired to spread her legs so he could* *place his wicked mouth on where she burned the* *hottest?*

It was bold. Wanton. Strictly forbidden.

Which was why she was going to allow His

Grace to take advantage of her. She no longer cared for society's dictates, her reputation . . . her heart.

She yearned for it.

"Really, Your Grace?" she goaded him, perching on the writing desk beside his quill and inkstand. She was a mass of jumbled thoughts, giddy and distracted by what was about to take place.

Was this where he conducted his affairs? Did he run his hands through his dark, sensible hair, ruffling it and his decorum when he managed his estate? Or did he untie his cravat and let the breeze cool his overheated skin?

"I am a man of my word." He approached her at the table. "And I make a point to keep my promises."

"What if you prove . . ." Emmaline cast a quick glance down to the jutting, straining outline in his breeches. "Unsatisfactory?"

The Duke was between her legs in a heartbeat. His eyes held her captive; his mouth hovered, a magnet, drawing her ever closer.

"Do not speak of what you do not know."

"Of what do I not know?" replied Emmaline, glancing back at him boldly even though her heart raced in her chest.

"How I will ride you so hard you will not mount your horse for a month if you continue your impertinence."

"I am not—"

His lips bruised in a kiss of carnal pleasure. She found herself scrambling, desperate to match his *need. Emmaline reached for his chest, feeling hard muscle beneath his waistcoat. She gasped when he drew back.*

"Not so fast, my sweet."

She blinked when he lifted her skirts, lowering himself between her legs as he undressed her. She opened her mouth to speak but was forestalled—his mouth had found that spot. She shivered as it burned from his hot breath.

"Your Grace!"

His head rose, eyes hot and heavy lidded. "Call me Maddern. This is what you want, is it not? To be used by a duke of considerable fortune?"

"You are a very misinformed man! I care not for your title or wealth."

"How about my cock . . . Do you care for it between your lips?"

She was dizzy, her stays impossibly tight, her need even tighter. She imagined his cock in her mouth. Was that what he meant? Surely not?

His hand, resting on the soft flesh of her thighs, moved closer. He looked up at her, eyes bright with wicked intent. A moment later, his fingers played along the wet folds of her most private part.

Emmaline shivered. Did he mean there?

The Duke's answering grin spoke volumes.

"Oh!" Emmaline moaned.

"You will allow me to take you . . . in amorous congress?"

"I . . . I . . ."

"Well?" he asked as he delved deeper.

"Yes," she cried out. "Oh yes!"

His mouth descended, teasing her, playful and adept. How many women had he sampled? How many had he tasted on his library table in this fashion?

She wondered at the sensations, the meeting of flesh to flesh, the spiraling of pleasure building and building until she could scarce draw breath. Emmaline panted, eyes closed, losing herself to him.

The spirals of need spun faster, ever faster, the dizzying delight carrying her beyond herself. The pressure of his hands on her thighs was punishing, but she jerked against his mouth, lost in whatever it was that was driving her to beg. She cared not, imploring him in sobbing gasps.

"More. Your Grace, I beg of—"

She broke. Shattered, as if she were rendered in two. It was a force that stunned her body and mind. Her pulse raced as she was caught in the rolling pleasure coursing through her. She could scarce draw breath.

As if emerging through the evening fog, the man beneath her came into view. She blinked, amazed. When he stood, a smile across his face, she could not contain her joy. Emmaline pressed her fingers to her lips, uncertain of the new sensation in her chest. It blossomed, growing in strength with every passing second.

She was floating on a cloud, impossibly relaxed.

And yet still eager for more. The heavy ache that pulsed between her thighs gave way to a new desire; a need buried deep inside, to be filled.

Savannah's heart thudded in her chest. Her eyes were heavy, her body burning for release. While she enjoyed imagining herself in the role of the heroine, she wondered what the Duke of Maddern would be thinking and feeling. What would he want from his lover?

Maddern reclined against the settee, watching the flush creep up Emmaline's cheeks. She was glowing, desirable, and all his.

He had lost her once. His own egregious error in judgement. But he was no longer a young blade, fresh out of Oxford, bound by his father's deception. Time had afforded him some sense and a chance to make amends.

He could only pray that she was amenable.

Headstrong. Bold. Impertinent.

The odds were unfavorable. And yet . . .

Maddern feasted on the sight before him. There was a thrill in knowing that he would have her now, after all these years. He could take what he wanted and to hell with the rules.

And right now, he wanted that soft mouth around his cock.

"*Kneel.*"

"*I beg your pardon, Your Grace?*"

"*Kneel, if you please, Miss Collins. I have a lesson I wish to teach you.*"

"*To teach me?*"

Maddern unbuttoned his breeches, freeing himself. He was proud of his length, as any man would be given the gift he had been bestowed. But it was his girth, the thick solid flesh that stretched across his erection, for which he was thankful. Not many men were built in such a fashion, nor knew how to wield it. Lord knew he had seen his fair share of cock in the men's baths and at the club, and he was smug in the knowledge that he lacked neither length nor girth. Smug still in the list of women who had been thoroughly satisfied by it. By him. He only hoped the sensual Miss Emmaline Collins proved fit for the task.

It would be a shame to be incompatible with the one woman who—

But now was not the time for sentiment, not when he was so close to losing control at the very sight of her: all that golden brown hair, curled and properly coiffured, her wide eyes, staring at him in innocent wonder, and her bosom, swelling above her dress, in search of an expert mouth to taste and plunder.

Emmaline's colour was high on her cheeks. With great satisfaction, he prided himself on having bestowed such pleasure on her, knowing he was the first, the only man to have touched her intimately.

"Is there a problem, Miss Collins?"

Her eyes shot to his. "Are all men this . . ." She gestured with her hands, mouth opening and closing like a fish out of water.

"Well endowed? I regret to inform you that I am on the larger end of the scale."

Emmaline licked her lips then gasped. He caught her arm, drawing her close. "I've something you can use that tongue on, sweetheart."

"But—what am I to do?"

"Like licking honey off a spoon, a few laps here and there, just at the tip." He pointed to the part of his cock straining and beginning to weep. "Touch it, if you dare."

She did, with a tentative finger, sinking down to her knees. "So warm."

"An inferno."

"And smooth."

"As silk. Unbearably hard too, so I suggest you take me in hand."

She frowned, her mouth pouting in confusion.

Maddern reached for her hands, guiding them up and down his length. They were small and soft and, after a few minutes, very skilled.

"Am I hurting you, Your Grace?"

"Maddern. Call me Maddern. And no." He gasped, looking down at her flushed face. "I am . . . Blazes!"

He was certain he would explode, caught be-

Virtue

tween the illicit nature of what she was doing and her innocence.

"Stop." He stayed his hand on hers, using the other to trace along the line of her breasts. "If you continue, I will not be able to control myself." He watched her bosom rise and fall. "Care to taste?" At her shy nod, he guided her head, instructing her. When her impertinent tongue licked at his beaded tip, he gnashed his teeth. He didn't dare frighten her or alert his guests.

Tentatively, then more boldly, she lapped at him, licking up and down his length just as he had taught her moments before.

"Now, open your mouth and take me in. Take me fully."

He need not guide her. The saucy innocent had figured it out, emboldened, no doubt by his praises, his sighs, his need for her.

When he felt his balls growing impossibly tight, Maddern shifted her.

"But—"

"Keep going. I'm close."

He groaned, urging her faster, pumping his cock in and out of her welcoming mouth. Then, with the pressure mounting to an impossible peak, he gripped her head and froze, coming in luxurious bursts.

Maddern barely heard her gasp as his blood rushed through his body, carrying with it any desire that had built up from moments before. For the moment.

"What is that?"

"My seed."

"Oh." Emmaline licked her lips. "It tastes —nice."

Maddern was surprised. He watched as she licked his cock slowly, mopping it up with her mouth.

She drew back, eyes mischievous. "You are salty and yet sweet."

Maddern's laughter tumbled out. "An accurate depiction of a man if I ever heard one."

Chapter Eleven

I t was late that night when Savannah was lying in bed, listening to the sounds of Arcas gaming, that the entry came to her. She debated on waiting until the morning, but finally logged on, dragging her laptop from her bedside table and fluffing the European pillow behind her for some extra support.

The ability to write about her sexual experiences was becoming easier. And much to her surprise, she was starting to have people comment on her entries. Strangers were reading her thoughts, sharing their own 'Sexcapades' and tips. Knowing they were interacting with her made the process doubly fun.

What had begun as a lark was fast becoming a fixation. Her thing.

Savannah began, giving herself up to the experience, drawing peace and purpose from the very act of journaling her thoughts.

It would be one entry then bed.

But not alone, never alone in her head. Not for the first time, she wondered about her favorite romance novel, about the elements of desire that fascinated her, preoccupying her thoughts. Not for the first time, she wondered if there was more to her sexuality that she hadn't yet explored.

Her understanding of herself, her needs . . . it was all there. But she was also still at the threshold of this new world of sexual discovery. There was so much more to experience.

Sitting up straighter, Savannah began.

Sexcapades - A Bucking Good Regency Romp

Sex starts in the mind. Isn't that what they say? It begins as a tantalizing call, a whisper or an image, a word that fires up the brain, arousing, calling to something many of us don't question: our innate, natural desire.

I love nothing more than fantasizing about sex in the nineteenth-century. The heated looks, stolen kisses, and downright archaic rules all serve one purpose: to make me hornier than an adolescent with a nudie magazine.

I can't help but fantasize about my favorite two characters: Emmaline Collins and William Barnet, the Duke of Maddern from *Love and Honor*. I picture myself as Emmaline getting bent over a table, skirts lifted as she's pounded from behind. I imagine her jerking off the

Duke in some remote corner of the estate, showing him her tits and letting him fondle her pussy.

I am hot for the forbidden nature of sex. So when I read books like *Love and Honor*, I can't stop myself from filling in all the naughty gaps. I find it the wildest turn-on, next to dirty talk. When my boyfriend pretends he's the Duke and I'm Emmaline while fucking me, the ride is even wilder.

If there were only a way to transport myself to the past, I'd do it. With my trusty Rabbit in hand, of course. And maybe a few whips and chains.

A sexy 9/10 on the O-meter.

Yours,

The Gamer's Girlfriend

 ⟨ ◦◦◦◦◦ ⟩

Savannah shut her laptop, grinning. With every entry, every new experience, she was making progress. And that progress was filling something inside of her she hadn't realized was missing. It was an odd sensation, unlike anything she had felt before.

And then it dawned on her, what it was that was happening.

It was an awakening. *Her* awakening.

One that would be life-changing, life-affirming . . . Life-giving.

Savannah was more than willing. Hell, she was fucking ready for it.

Also By Ida Brady

The Gamer's Girlfriend Series

Book 1

Virtue

Book 2

Voyeur

Book 3

Vixen

Teacher Chronicles Series

Before You Were Mine

When You Were Mine

If You Were Mine (Coming 2023)

A Sweet, Sexy, Scandalous Series

Sweet Spot

Sex and the Stage

Secrets and Scandals

Standalones

To Tango with Love

About the Author

Ida Brady writes contemporary romance novels that promise humour, heartbreak and a happily ever after. With all the sexy bits! A lover of chocolate (milk or dark) and thunderstorms (the bigger the better), she's usually dreaming about her next cast of characters or what she's going to eat for her next meal. When she isn't trying to tame her intractable curls, she's running after her kids, usually with a book in hand.

Ida lives in Melbourne with her Irish husband and their out-of-control collection of books. She sometimes daydreams about having a huge library in her apartment but will settle for stacking novels in the kitchen drawers instead. In her past life, she taught VCE Literature and English to a gaggle of teenagers. While she misses their enthusiasm, she sure as hell doesn't miss marking papers. You might find her dancing the sexy Argentine tango in her spare time, which isn't very often these days. She loves travelling with her family, observing strangers at café's, and getting lost in a good story.

Want to hear more?

Visit: http://www.idabrady.com or sign up to my

Newsletter, With You in Romance for giveaways
and prizes!
Follow me on Tiktok, Facebook! and Instagram or
leave a review on Goodreads.

SUBSCRIBE FOR ALL THE NEWS!
If you want exclusive access to giveaways, sales, and
new release alerts first, then subscribe to my
monthly newsletter, With You in Romance at
www.idabrady.com

Acknowledgments

I have to start by thanking Brian for encouraging me to write this series. Without you and your unwavering support, I might never have had the courage to give it a red-hot go. And babe, I'm so happy I did. So thank you for reminding me to be true to my creativity, and for supporting me, always. Love you sooo much, B!

So this series has been percolating in my brain for a while, and it just wouldn't go away. Naturally, I changed my release schedule so that I could write The Gamer's Girlfriend instead of a different series, and I'm so damn glad I did.

This has been an equally tough but fun series to write. I have loved these characters from the moment they've popped into my head. I know, I know, I say that about every book, but it's true! I've been a lover of historical romance for a very long time, and I wanted to do it justice, so I hope that this lives up to your expectations.

So, on to formal thank yous.

To Team Brida: Brian, Adria, Niamh and Hugo. I can say I'm the luckiest woman in the world to have you all in my corner. All that love and support, not to mention sweet little hugs, have kept this sleep-deprived mamma going when some days it was just bloody tough. Love you all to the moon and back!

To Hilary, my Alpha reader and friend. I know, without a shadow of a doubt, that this series wouldn't be where it is today without your brutally honest feedback. Your advice, support and wealth of knowledge has made me strive to really better myself and my work. I can't thank you enough for everything, and I am still gushing over your initial reaction to reading it. Honestly, it's those moments that keep me going when this all feels so hard. So thank you!! Dinner is on me.

To Norma Gambini, you remain a treasure to work with. Thank you so much for your editing prowess. I'm so luck that I get to work with you. Like I always say, you're the best!

To Tash, a million thank yous for all the wonderful work on my covers. I cannot gush over them enough. You have a gift!!

To Ebony, formatter guru and all-around awesome person. Thanks SO much for all your work over the years. You're a gem to work with and an absolute life-saver on those deadlines.

To my family, as always for the love and support both near and across the wild Atlantic.

To my wonderful writer friends, my Meetup girls, your advice, feedback and general support really makes me feel like I can do this. I wouldn't be where I am without your friendship and support, so thank you! Here's to another release, and hopefully another retreat down the track!

To my BETA readers, once again, your time, effort and insight make me feel super lucky to have you all in my life. Thank you for all the feedback, encouragement, and support. Y'all ROCK!

Finally, to my readers. Whoever you are, wherever you may be, I hope that this novel gives you a chance to escape from reality, even if for a chapter or two.

With you in romance,

Ida Brady

www.ingramcontent.com/pod-product-compliance
Lightning Source LLC
Chambersburg PA
CBHW030416120726
47904CB00007B/2302

* 9 7 8 0 6 4 5 4 1 8 6 6 8 *